TWO TIME LOSER
DETECTIVE STORIES

Steve D.!
broof!

by

Tim Wall

duck! +
duck!
goose!

Watermill Press

Illustrations by Jim Odbert

ISBN 0-89375-746-2

CONTENTS

Ask Me No Questions

Maureen Brett came to see me on a Monday afternoon.

"Are you Mike London, the detective?" she asked.

"That's right," I said. She had stepped into my office. "What can I do to help you?"

"I don't know," she said. She looked at me and tried to smile. "I mean, I hope you can help me, but I don't know what should be done. You'll have to excuse me if I don't say the right things. I've never gone to a detective before."

"That's all right," I said. "Some people go through their whole lives without hiring a detective. Why don't you just tell me what the problem is?"

"It's about my husband," she said. "He's been worried about something for weeks. I've asked him what the trouble is, but he won't answer. I just can't get him to tell me what's bothering him."

"That is a problem, Mrs. Brett," I said. "However, marriage counseling is a little out of my line of business."

"Please let me finish, Mr. London," she said. "Last Friday, I looked through all of my husband's belongings.

Jeffrey—that's my husband—was at work. I felt awful searching through my husband's things, but I didn't know what else to do. I found this note."

Mrs. Brett took a small, square envelope out of her purse. There was a note inside. It said:

Tuesday night at eleven o'clock in front of O'Malley's. Bring five hundred dollars in cash.

"I worried about it the entire weekend," said Mrs. Brett. "Finally, I decided to come to this detective agency."

"You did the right thing, Mrs. Brett," I said. "This doesn't look good. Give me a few days to come up with something." She was on her way out when I stopped her. "There's one more thing. I'll need a

Mrs. Brett took a small, square envelope out of her purse.

picture of your husband."

She reached into her wallet and handed me a snapshot. It was her wedding photo.

After she left, I planned what I would do. Someone was trying to blackmail Jeffrey Brett. If he wouldn't tell his wife about it, he certainly wouldn't tell me. But, if I could find out who showed up to meet Jeffrey Brett, I'd have something to go on.

So, I drove out to O'Malley's on Tuesday night. I made sure to get there by ten-thirty, half an hour before the time mentioned in the note.

O'Malley's is at the edge of town. It's a lonely spot. The railroad yards are across the street. Next door is a deserted building. One of the boards over the windows of the building appeared to be loose.

A big, heavy man walked past O'Malley's.

I pulled the board off and stepped inside the window. From there, I could watch what happened without being seen.

Fifteen minutes before eleven o'clock, a big, heavy man walked past O'Malley's. He stopped in front of the building I was hiding in. He was so close, I could have reached out and touched him.

It looked as though I wasn't the only one who was keeping a watch on Jeffrey Brett's meeting.

At eleven, another man came down the sidewalk. As he passed under a street lamp, I saw that it was Jeffrey Brett. He stopped in front of the alley between O'Malley's and the deserted building.

Brett didn't have to wait long. A small man stepped out of O'Malley's. He wore a hat pulled low over his face and walked over to Brett. He said something I couldn't hear. Then, I saw Brett hand over a package to the man. That would be the money.

They talked some more. Then Brett's voice grew louder.

"You said you'd give them to me!" Brett yelled. "Hand them over!" He reached out his hands and went for the little man's neck.

Then, the big man in front of me moved in. He'd probably been sent there in case Brett tried to get rough. He walked up to Brett from behind.

I jumped over the window sill and followed the big man onto the sidewalk. With my pistol in my hand, I clubbed him on the back of the neck. He fell to the ground. The little guy was so surprised that he dropped the package. Naturally, I scooped it up right away.

I saw Brett hand over a package to the man.

By this time, the little guy saw that things weren't going very well. He ran off down the street.

I handed Brett the package. "I think this belongs to you."

"You sure came along at the right time, mister," Brett said to me.

I steered Brett into O'Malley's. He was still shaken up from all the excitement, and it wasn't hard for me to get him to talk.

"You see, it wasn't too long ago that I was in jail," he explained. "I served three years for armed robbery. After I did my time, I moved out here. It was hard enough to get a job, even without a record. So I changed my name. Then I met a girl, and we got married.

"Everything was fine until I ran into someone from my home town. You saw the man. He was the little guy with the hat. He knew who I was, of course, and he noticed I had changed my name.

"I told him I didn't want my wife to know about my past. That was a mistake. He found some newspaper clippings describing my arrest. They showed my picture with my old name. He told me he would send them to my wife if I didn't pay him."

"So what?" I asked. "Why not let him send them?"

"You don't know my wife. She's a good woman. She comes from a different background than I do. If she finds out, I wouldn't blame her for leaving me."

"You're a fool twice over," I said. "First, for paying blackmail. Even if they had given you those clippings, they would have kept a copy. They know that if you pay once, you'll pay

"If my wife finds out, I wouldn't blame her for leaving me."

again. After what happened tonight, you can be sure they'll be back to ask for the money. And they'll be angry enough to ask for twice as much.

"Second, you're a fool for not telling your wife. If she's as good as you say she is, she won't care about your background."

"How can you be so sure?" he asked.

"I have a feeling for these things," I told him. "Look, it's late. You should be home, and so should I. Go back and tell your wife your story. After that, if those blackmailers show up again, you can just laugh at them."

The next day, Mrs. Brett called me at the office.

"I can't thank you enough, Mr. London," she said. "Jeff and I talked for a long time last night. I told him he was crazy to think that his past mistakes would change anything between us. He told me about the friendly stranger who helped him out and gave him advice. I didn't let on that I knew who the stranger was."

"Fine," I said. "We'll keep it that way."

"There's one thing you were wrong about, though," she said.

"What was that?" I wondered.

"You were wrong when you said that marriage counseling was out of your line. I think you'd do fine as a marriage counselor."

I'll keep that in mind, in case the detective business ever slows up.

The Black Bag Job

I've been a detective for fifteen years, and I like to work alone. It's better that way. Things go faster, and I don't have to worry about my partner making a mistake.

But this time, I knew I would need some help. I decided to call Freddy

Malone, an old friend of mine.

He answered his phone on the first ring.

"Hello, Freddy," I said. "This is Mike London. Long time, no see. How have you been?"

"Not so well," he said. "It's tough being out of work. It's not just the money, you understand. It does something to your pride."

I said, "Yeah, it must be rough."

"It's these new safes," Freddy went on. "They make them with electronic time-locks now. The only way to crack them is to blow them up. That's not my field. I'm strictly a touch man, you know?"

"They don't call you 'Fingers' for nothing," I said. "I have a job for you. Are you interested?"

"You know I am," he said. "You won't

be sorry, Mike. When you work with 'Fingers' Malone, you're working with a pro."

"Fine," I said. "I'll pick you up tonight at twelve o'clock. All right?"

We agreed on a meeting place and hung up.

When I met Freddy, later that night, he wore an overcoat and carried his little black bag of tools.

I headed the car to Glenmere. Glenmere is a quiet, well-to-do neighborhood outside of town. I explained the job to Freddy as I drove.

"Our detective agency has been hired by a Mr. Robinson," I said. "Robinson had a business partner. After a while, Robinson noticed that his partner was cheating him. So Robinson quit the company. But when he tried to get his money out of the business, the partner

21

*"When you work with 'Fingers' Malone,
you're working with a pro."*

took him to court.

"Robinson says there are papers which will prove his side of the story. But his partner, a man called Gilmore, has the only copy of the file. The file is kept in a safe in Gilmore's house."

"So you want to get the file, and you want me to crack the safe," Freddy finished up for me.

"That's it," I said.

"Gilmore's safe isn't one of those new jobs, is it?" Freddy asked. He sounded worried.

"No," I said. "It's an old-fashioned wall safe. I went out to Gilmore's house, in Glenmere, to talk with him. I couldn't get anything out of him, but I got a look at the safe."

When we got to Glenmere, I parked a few blocks from Gilmore's house. We walked the rest of the way. I led Freddy into some bushes on the side of the Gilmore house. We peeked into a dark window that looked into the study, where the safe was.

I started to lift the window sash. Freddy held back my hand.

"The alarm," he whispered. He pointed to a wire that traced the side of the window.

He rummaged around in his bag and brought out a small screwdriver. He found the place where the wires connected and took out the screws. Then, he used a small knife to open the catch on the window.

When we were in the study, I switched on my flashlight, shading the beam with my hand. I played the beam along the wall until I found the safe.

Freddy brought more tools out of his bag. One of the tools was a stethoscope.

I led Freddy into some bushes on the side of the Gilmore house.

He put the ends of the stethoscope into his ears and placed the wide metal part against the safe. I held the flashlight, while he listened through the stethoscope and worked the knob of the safe with his fingers.

Two minutes later, the door of the safe clicked open. I pulled out the papers from inside the safe and held them under my light. I put the ones I needed into my coat pocket.

"A piece of cake," Freddy breathed into my ear.

It would have been, too, if Freddy hadn't bumped into a lamp as we went out the window. It went over with a crash. We heard steps overhead.

Quickly, we climbed out the window and ran through the bushes in Gilmore's yard. When we came to the sidewalk, we started toward my car.

Then we heard the scream of a police car. As we neared my car, flashing lights appeared around the corner.

Freddy turned to me. I thought he was going to tell me something. That's why my chin was hanging out when he took a swing. He punched me right in the jaw. Stunned, I fell to the sidewalk.

What happened next isn't all that clear to me. I was stretched out, flat on my back. There was the sound of a car pulling up. Red and white lights flashed in my eyes. Looking up, I saw Freddy kneeling over me.

A policeman got out of the car. "What's going on here?" I remember him saying. I noticed that my shirt had been pulled open. Freddy was holding something cold and hard against my chest. The stethoscope!

"I found this man passed out on the

"What's going on here?"

street, Officer," I heard Freddy say.

"Do you want us to take him to a hospital?" the policeman asked.

I groaned.

"That won't be necessary," Freddy said. "He's waking up."

"All right, Doctor," the policeman said. "If you're sure. We're busy ourselves right now. We're looking for someone who broke into a house up the street."

The police car pulled away. I sat up. The stethoscope was still hanging from Freddy's ears. His little black bag was next to him on the sidewalk.

"That was quick thinking," I said, rubbing my jaw.

"I told you," Freddy said. "When you work with 'Fingers' Malone, you're working with a pro."

The Manswood Killing

George Manswood was very old and very rich. One night, he was taking a walk outside his house, and someone shot him. His body was found on the lawn, near the edge of the woods that surrounded his house.

Three days later, Mrs. Manswood called our detective agency. The police still hadn't found the killer. She was tired of seeing her family's name in the newspapers. She wanted our agency to find the person who had killed her husband.

I drove out to see Mrs. Manswood the next day.

The Manswood house is out in the country. The only address I had been given was "Birdtree Lane," and the directions I had weren't much help. After an hour of driving around in circles, I knew I was lost. Finally, I stopped at a small gas station.

It was a funny little place. The gas pumps were the rounded, old-fashioned kind. Someone had shot two wild ducks and hung them up over the door.

An old man was painting the front of

*Someone had shot two wild ducks and
hung them up over the door.*

the station. When I drove up, he limped out to my car.

"How do you get to Birdtree Lane?" I asked him.

He looked at me, then at my car. "Are you from the city?" he asked me.

I nodded.

He stared at the sky for a second.

"Business has been real slow lately," he said. "I've had hardly any customers. Now, you come out here wanting free information."

I pulled out a dollar. He folded it and slipped it into his shirt pocket.

"You just passed Birdtree Lane," he said. "It's that dirt road over there."

I started to put the car into gear.

"You'll be going out to the Manswood house then," he continued.

"Could be," I replied.

"Then you could be looking into how

Manswood got himself killed," said the old man.

"Could be," I agreed.

He looked at the sky again.

This time I pulled out a twenty-dollar bill. He put it in the same pocket with the other bill.

"Manswood was shot with a .22, right?" he said. "A while back, I was out at his house to fix the car. There's a .22 in the shed in the back of the house. You might want to ask his wife about that. You can figure out for yourself how much money she's going to get now that he's dead."

I drove the car back onto the road and turned up the lane. Half a mile farther, a large brick house stood in the middle of a rolling lawn and flowering bushes. This was the Manswood house. Thick forest surrounded it.

This was the Manswood house.

A servant answered the door. Mrs. Manswood was expecting me, he said. He showed me to the living room.

Mrs. Manswood was dressed in black, but she didn't look like she had been doing any crying lately. She sat in a red velvet chair, her back stiff and straight.

I asked her the usual questions. Mrs. Manswood had one son. He lived in South America. The servants had had the day off on Saturday, the day Manswood had been shot.

"Your husband was a rich man, Mrs. Manswood," I said. "Did he have any enemies?"

"He was a hard man, Mr. London," she said. "All his old business associates were enemies. But Mr. Manswood stopped working several years ago. None of his old business associates are still alive."

"So, his primary interests for the last few years have been the house and the grounds?" I asked.

"That's all," Mrs. Manswood said. "Except for all this business about a superhighway."

"What business is that?" I asked.

Mrs. Manswood waved a thin, wrinkled hand in the air. "They've been planning one of those awful highways to cut across Birdtree Lane. Of course, Mr. Manswood wouldn't stand for it. It would have ruined his peace and quiet. He used all his power to keep it from being built. Now that he's gone, it will probably be built anyway."

"One more question, Mrs. Manswood. Did your husband often take walks around the grounds?"

"He went out every afternoon, without fail," she said.

*"My husband went out every afternoon,
without fail."*

I excused myself and went outside. I stopped at the spot where Manswood had been shot. But I only looked around for a moment. If there had been anything there, the police would have already found it. I was more interested in the shed that the old man at the gas station had told me about.

I found the gun in a corner of the shed. I snapped it open and looked down the barrel. It was rusty and blocked with dirt. If you tried to shoot somebody with it, it would probably blow up in your hands.

I used Mrs. Manswood's phone to call the local chief of police. I told him I had been hired to help find Manswood's killer.

"Manswood was shot with a .22," I said.

"Yep," he agreed. "In the back. While

he was walking around his land."

"But you haven't said anything about the .22 to the papers, have you?" I asked.

"No. I've wanted to wait until I had more to go on. Have you come up with any ideas?"

"Maybe. I'll let you know."

I told Mrs. Manswood I would send her a report. On my way back to the highway, I stopped at the gas station.

The old man was still painting. He came over when I hit my horn.

"I'm interested in those ducks," I said.

The old man nodded. "They'd make a mighty good meal. You can't get them fresh like that in the city. I could let you have one for the right price."

"That's not why I'm interested in them," I said. "Did you shoot those ducks yourself?"

The old man's eyes narrowed. "What of it?" he asked.

"I'll bet you used a .22," I said. "A .22 is a good bird gun. You must do a lot of hunting. Of course, most of the land in these parts belongs to Manswood. You must be in his woods often. You must have seen him take his walks."

"Say, who are you? The game warden?" he sneered.

I went on as if I hadn't heard him. "You're painting your station, I see. This place will be pretty valuable when they put the new highway through. It's lucky for you that Manswood is out of the way. Or is it just luck?" I asked with a smile.

"You'll have to explain what you're talking about, mister." The old guy was getting scared.

"What of it?" the old man asked.

"You made a mistake," I said, "when you told me about the .22 in Manswood's shed. No one but the police chief knew Manswood was shot with a .22. No one, that is, but the chief and the murderer."

I had my gun out from under my coat before he could get away.

"Have a seat, mister," I said. "I need someone to give me directions to the police station."

TWO TIME LOSER

No two investigations are ever the same. This time, I was hired to find a bank robber. The man I wanted was Jake Hanratty. He had already done time for a bank job in St. Louis. They called him "Cousin Jake" out there.

The Madison Savings and Loan

Bank had been held up the month before. We received a tip connecting Jake with the stick-up. Now, the Madison bank was one of our customers. They wanted us to find Jake. If possible, they wanted their money back, too.

According to our files, Jake was a big man. He had curly, black hair and small, green eyes. He liked to wear bright shirts, well-tailored suits, and flashy rings. He had last been seen on the other side of town, down by the tracks, so I decided to have a look around.

I spent a day checking the rooming houses and hotels in that part of town. Jake Hanratty wasn't registered in any of them.

But I knew the man had to eat. I started checking out all the restaurants in the neighborhood. Then, after two

According to our files, Jake was a big man.

days, I got a break.

I was at a place called Pierre's, when a couple came in and sat down at a table.

The man was tall and broad-shouldered, with black hair and green eyes. A ring flashed on his finger when he pulled out a chair for the girl. She had a pale face, a small mouth, and yellow hair.

A waiter went over to take their order.

"Two steaks, the biggest you have," the man said loudly. "Salad, peas, potatoes, the works. And anything else the lady wants."

I sipped my coffee, trying to make it last. After they finished eating, the man paid the bill. He left a big tip.

I followed them out into the street. They climbed into a black Chevy. The number on the back was TUX-547.

I ducked into a cab. The Chevy went

around the block and headed north. Soon, it parked in front of the Vanderbilt Hotel.

I paid my driver, then waited a minute. As I entered the hotel, I saw them get into the elevator. I watched the light above the elevator doors. It stopped at the eighth floor.

I walked up to the desk. "I'd like something for the night," I told the clerk.

"Certainly," the clerk said as he turned the book around for me to sign my name.

I glanced at the page. Room 842 was under the name of "Mr. and Mrs. Smith." That's all I needed to know.

"I want a room with a view of the river," I demanded.

The clerk stared at me. "The river? Are you kidding? The river is two miles

*The Chevy went around the block
and headed north.*

from here."

"What?" I asked. "No view of the river? Do you expect me to stay in a room without a view? What kind of person do you take me for?" I turned and walked out the door.

The next morning, I called the detective agency office. Fast Freddy Rapillo answered the phone.

"Look up a car with the number TUX-547," I said. "Call me as soon as you get something. I'm at my room."

Rapillo called back two hours later. That's why we call him Fast Freddy.

"The car belongs to Gloria Newhouse," he reported.

"OK," I said. "Look Gloria up in the files. Let me know what you find."

I settled down with a magazine. Freddy phoned back at one o'clock.

"Gloria is in trouble," he said. "She's

wanted for a couple of bad checks in St. Louis."

I said thanks and hung up.

Now, I could have been a great detective. I could have followed Gloria and Jake for the next two months. I could have gone back to the bank and talked to the people who saw the stick-up. I could have done a lot of things.

However, I just didn't have time to be a great detective. I was paid to get things done—the sooner, the better.

That's why I went back to the Vanderbilt Hotel. I kept watch in front of a newspaper stand.

An hour later, the big guy came out, looking up and down the street. Then, he headed toward the corner.

I went up to Room 842 and knocked on the door. The girl answered.

I stepped inside. "It's all over, Gloria,"

I said. "I know about those bad checks you wrote in St. Louis. Of course, I could forget about them, if you tell me what you know about the Madison bank robbery."

Gloria turned a few shades paler than she already was.

It wasn't long before I had the facts I needed.

"I'll see to it that you get a break," I said. "But you've got to do something else for me. Bring Jake to the restaurant downstairs at six o'clock sharp."

Later that evening, Paul Boone, another detective from the agency, met me at the hotel. At six o'clock, we were by the door of the restaurant.

Gloria and the big guy came walking in.

"Cousin Jake," I called out. The big man turned toward me.

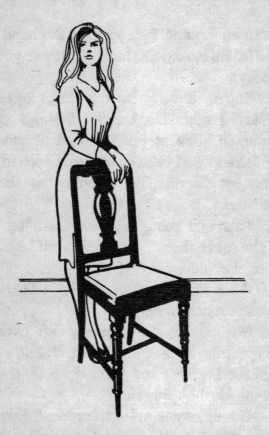

*Gloria turned a few shades paler
than she already was.*

In an instant, I slapped on the hand-cuffs. He looked like he might try to get rough.

"You're already a one-time loser, Jake," I said. "Don't make it rough on yourself." Paul stepped in front of him.

Jake looked hard at me for a second, then at Gloria. Gloria looked at the ground.

"This was going to be my last job," Jake said to her. "I thought that if I had you, I could go straight."

Gloria didn't say anything. There wasn't much to say.

"Do you have any money left over from this little honeymoon, Jake?" I asked. I wasn't too thrilled about the whole deal by this time.

"The money is up in the room," Jake said. "It's in my bag. It won't do me any good now." His big shoulders dropped under his light gray coat and purple shirt.

"Come on, Jake, let's go," I said. "You're making me cry."

Bright Lights, Big City

One Friday night, I ran into the Oklahoma Kid. It was a misty night, and a light rain was falling. I was walking down the street, and the Kid was walking in the other direction, staring up in the air.

We met in the center of the sidewalk.

The Kid was staring up in the air.

Actually, the Kid walked right into me, lost his balance, and fell. I helped him up as quickly as I could. I was in a hurry to move on. I was in the middle of a case.

I had been following "Rembrandt" Shultz, the counterfeiter. He was wanted for some bad hundreds he had been printing.

"Excuse me," I said to the Kid. I could see the back of Shultz's square head disappearing into the crowd.

"Excuse *me,* sir," said the Kid. "It was my fault."

"Nothing to worry about," I said. I tried to hurry past him, but he had grabbed me by both arms.

"You know, you're the first person who has spoken to me since I came to this city," he said. "Maybe you can tell me where Betty Lou is."

By this time, Shultz was gone. I stared at the boy. "Betty Lou?" I asked. That could have been my first mistake.

"That's right, Betty Lou Harris. Do you know her? We're going to be married."

"There are a few million people in this city, son. Even if I did know a Betty Lou, I don't think it would be the one you're looking for. Anyway, you're the one that's marrying her, not me."

I turned to go, but he held me tight.

"Betty and I decided we would get married, while we were still in Oklahoma," the Kid explained. "She came here because she was offered a job, and we needed the money. She was going to send me her address as soon as she got settled. Then I had to leave the place where I was staying in an awful hurry." He kicked the ground with his big toe.

"The way things were, I couldn't leave a forwarding address," he mumbled.

"That's fine," I said. "You just keep walking up and down these streets. She's sure to turn up. Now I'm going home. I've got a lot of detective work to do tomorrow."

Telling him that I was a detective was my second mistake. Or maybe it was my third. It seemed that every time I opened my mouth, it got worse.

"You're a detective, mister?" the Kid smiled. "Why you're just the type of fellow I need to find my Betty Lou."

He was beside himself with joy, jumping around like a big dog. And he was still holding on to my arms.

I asked him a few questions about Betty Lou. That seemed to be the only way I would ever get back home that night.

He told me that Betty Lou was a waitress at a club somewhere in the center of town. All the Kid knew about the place was that it had blue lighting and a seven-piece band. I recognized it right away.

"That'll be the Monte Carlo," I said. "It's just a few blocks from here. I'll show you."

A few minutes later, the name "Monte Carlo" glowed in blue lights up ahead. I nodded to the doorman as we walked inside.

The next thing I knew, the Kid was hooting like a cowboy. "Betty Lou!" The girl looked up, and, in a flash, they were in each other's arms. Betty Lou must have missed him as much as he had missed her.

Now was my chance to leave. With luck, I'd be home in half an hour. As I

He told me that Betty Lou was a waitress at a club.

turned to go, I bumped into one of the tables. I started to say I was sorry. Then I saw that big, square face.

"Well, well, Rembrandt," I chuckled. "Nice to see you again."

Shultz knew me from several years ago. We weren't exactly friends. As he reached into his coat, I dived at him across the table. Shultz pushed me over, and the table came with me. The hum of voices in the club stopped. A woman screamed.

As I rolled over, I saw Shultz aiming a gun at my head. I rolled in the other direction.

When I looked up again, the Kid was on top of Shultz. In two seconds, Rembrandt was knocked out cold. He never knew what hit him. The Kid had saved me a lot of work.

I smoothed out my suit. "You know,

Shultz reached into his coat.

kid," I said, "they had a reward out on this guy. Half of it is yours. The money might help you and Betty Lou get started."

The Kid shook my hand. "Mister, this is truly cause to celebrate. You and Betty Lou and me..."

"Oh no," I said. "I'm taking Rembrandt to the station. And then I'm getting some sleep."

In this business, you have to quit while you're ahead.

Trouble at the Palace Hotel

"Ten of our guests have been robbed within the last month," Herbert Swanson said. Swanson was the manager of the Palace Hotel. "That's why I called your detective agency, Mr. London. The Palace is a first-class hotel. We can't afford to get a bad name."

"Your house detective, Vogel, is a pretty good man," I said. "He's done some favors for me in the past. What does he think?"

Swanson shook his head. "Vogel hasn't come up with anything. Between you and me, I don't think he's the right man for the job. I'm planning to let him go. But for now, I need to protect our guests. I'm giving the job to you."

After I finished talking with the manager, I went to see Vogel, the house detective.

Vogel's office was behind the lobby. His desk was pushed against one wall. The back of Vogel's chair was pushed against the other. And Vogel's stomach was pressed against the desk. I sat on the desk.

"Well, well, if it isn't Mike London," Vogel said.

Vogel gave me a pained look.

I asked him what he thought about the robberies.

"It looks to me like it's one person doing all the robberies," Vogel said. "He, or she, must have a passkey. The thief knows which guests have money. He knows when they're in and when they're out. There's no sign of the doors or windows being forced."

"I suppose you checked out any strangers hanging out in the lobby," I said.

Vogel gave me a pained look. "Of course. I didn't get into this business yesterday."

"And the maids?" I asked.

"They check out as far as I can tell. I've known most of them for years. I think they're OK."

I gave Vogel my ideas, and together we worked out a plan. I went out the back way so I wouldn't draw any attention to myself.

First, I visited a jeweler who owed me a favor. He loaned me a couple of fancy leather cases and a diamond tie pin.

I returned to the Palace and checked in at the desk under the name "Markham." Vogel had set aside the best room in the hotel for me. With the leather cases and the tie pin, I looked like a man who had a lot of money. I did my best to act the part.

I gave the bellboy a big tip. I pulled the bills from a large roll, making sure he could see it.

After I was settled, I went downstairs to the hotel gift shop. I picked out a few things I liked, and paid for them with a large bill.

I went back to my room and put the things away. I walked to the window and opened it. I could see where the fire escape dropped to a back alley.

I felt I had made a good start. It was time for dinner. I made sure the window was still open, and then went downstairs.

They have a nice dining room at the Palace. The lights are low, the music is soft. I ordered a steak dinner.

I had just started on the steak when the man at the next table spoke in a loud voice. He was saying that the waiter brought him the wrong dish. The waiter stood by the table, looking at the floor. The young man insulted him in slow, even sentences. The people at the near-by tables had stopped talking, but they were trying not to notice.

Finally, the young man got up and walked away. He didn't even ask for a check. He was wearing a light pink jacket and had a scarf tied around his neck.

When the waiter passed by my table, I reminded him to bring my coffee.

"You want to tell me anything else I forgot?" he growled.

"Yeah," I said. "You forgot that I'm not the one who insulted you. It was the other guy."

He looked at me hard for a second, then grinned.

"I guess I shouldn't have let him get under my skin. I feel a little foolish."

"Forget it. Who is he?" I asked.

"Arthur Swanson." When I raised my eyebrows, he said, "That's right, the manager's son. I wouldn't have let anyone else talk to me that way. But I have to be careful with him. The old man thinks his son can do no wrong. The kid spends all his time hanging around his father's hotel. Old Man Swanson lets him get away with it."

When I went out to the lobby, the Swanson kid was still there. He was talking to a young woman.

I flashed a bill at the doorman and asked him to flag down a cab. A taxi pulled up to the curb, and I climbed in.

When the cab driver had turned the corner, I told her to let me off.

"Is this some kind of a joke, mister?" she asked.

I gave her a few extra dollars for her trouble. I really hadn't wanted to go anywhere. I just wanted it to look as though I would be away for a while.

I got out of the cab and found the alley that runs behind the Palace. The alley led to the fire escape. I stood on top of a garbage can and climbed up to the fire escape's lowest platform.

A taxi pulled up to the curb, and I climbed in.

I walked up the steps, counting the floors, until I was level with my room. Then, I stepped through the window I had left open.

A detective spends more time waiting than doing anything else. At least, this time, I wasn't standing on a corner in the rain. I felt for a chair in the dark and set it next to the door. I sat down. Then I waited.

I figured the thief was someone who kept a close watch on all the guests at the hotel. He would have seen what a big spender I was, and figured I had valuables and money in my room. He probably saw me leave the hotel, and would have guessed I'd be out on the town for most of the night. However, when he came to rob my room, I'd be waiting for him.

It was a great plan. After a few hours

of waiting, I wondered if it would work.

At twelve-thirty, I heard a click at the door. As the door opened, dim light streamed in. A figure walked into the room. Then, the door closed, and it was dark again.

Some moments passed, and neither of us moved. Then a thin beam of light snapped on. It played over the room and stopped by the night table next to my bed.

The circle of light became smaller as the figure walked toward the night table. Without a sound, I stepped to the light switch and turned on the lights.

The man whirled around. He wore a pink jacket and a knotted scarf. He was about to rush for the door.

I swung at his jaw, and he fell over backward onto the bed. While he was still unconscious, I took the scarf from

A figure walked into the room.

his neck. Then I went into the bathroom and got a glass of cold water. I threw the water on his face, and he woke up. I told him to get out so I could get some sleep.

The next morning, I went to see the manager.

I told him what had happened. At first, he didn't believe what I said about his son. When I threw Arthur's scarf on the table, he looked as if I had punched him in the stomach.

"Your son was always in the hotel," I explained. "He knew when the guests were out of their rooms. He could walk into your office and no one would have given it a second thought. He easily could have taken a passkey, and then made a copy of it."

Swanson had turned around so he didn't have to look at me. "Do we have to take this to the police?" he finally asked.

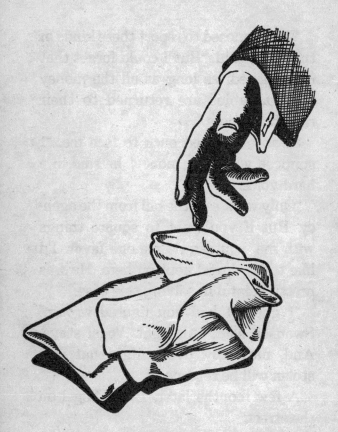

I threw Arthur's scarf on the table.

"I'm supposed to report these kinds of things," I said. "But I could forget that it happened, as long as all the money and valuables are returned to their rightful owners."

Swanson turned back to face me. "I suppose you want money," he said in a hard voice.

"Only what's on the bill from the agency. But if you want to square things with me, you can do me one favor. I'd like to see Vogel kept on here. He was pretty helpful in solving this case."

"I guess I had you figured wrong," Swanson said. "All right. Vogel stays. And, naturally, everything that was stolen will be returned."

A few months later, I met Vogel on the street.

"How's our old friend Arthur Swanson doing?" I asked.

Vogel grinned. "He's doing fine. After what happened, his old man told him he'd have to get a job, but neither of them knew what he could do. Then his father decided that, since Arthur Swanson had been such a smart crook, he'd probably make a great detective."

Vogel winked. "Now he's on my staff. I'm training him in the detective business."

The Case of the Lucky Nephew

One morning, when I got to my office, a man was waiting to see me. He was from the law firm of Gridley, Gridley, Harmon, and Finch.

"I'll get right to the point, Mr. London," he said. "Our firm of lawyers is handling the estate of a Mr. Milford Huntington. Last month, he died. He left a good deal of money as well as stock in the family business. His only living relative is a nephew, Benny Golson. All we know about Mr. Golson is that he's been living in this city for the last ten years. He hasn't been in touch with his uncle.

"The letters we've sent Mr. Golson have been returned without a forwarding address. Our law offices are two hundred miles from here. We've hired your detective agency to find Mr. Golson so he can get in touch with us. Your manager told me you could handle the job."

He took a letter from his pocket. "This letter explains everything," he said. "Give it to Mr. Golson when you find him."

The job seemed simple enough. The last known address for Benny Golson was the Holiday Home Motel. I decided to try there first. Someone at the motel might know where Golson had gone.

I drove out to the Holiday Home Motel. It was on the highway outside of town. There was a main office and a row of small wooden cabins. I went into the office.

I asked the lady behind the desk if she knew where I could find Benny Golson. "I'd like to find him also," she said. "He skipped out three months ago. He still owes me three months' rent."

"Do you know anything else about him?" I asked. "Who his friends were? Who he worked for?"

"Besides not paying his rent," she answered, "I only remember one thing about him. He sold me two tickets to the

*The motel was on the highway
outside of town.*

Firefighters' Ball."

"That was nice of him," I said.

"No it wasn't. The fire department didn't hold a ball that year."

I was starting to get the idea that Benny Golson might not be a very honest person. I found a pay phone and called a friend who worked on the police force.

I asked him about Benny.

"Sure, we know him," he said. "We've been watching him. We think he's part of a gang that steals watches and jewelry. He sells the hot watches from a laundromat on Fifth Street."

I got back into my car and drove downtown. I parked a few blocks from Fifth Street and walked to the laundromat.

Two ladies with their hair in rollers were folding their wash. A kid in the back of the laundromat seemed to be in charge.

When I walked up to the kid, he pulled a gold watch from his pocket.

"How would you like to buy a nice watch for twenty dollars?" he asked.

I shook my head. "I'm looking for Benny Golson."

The kid acted as though he had never heard the name before.

"Golson, Golson," he repeated. "Sorry, mister. I don't know any Golson."

"I've got some news he'll want to hear," I said.

"Sorry, mister," the boy said. "I can't help you."

I figured the kid thought that Golson owed me money, or that I was from the police. He wasn't going to tell me anything. But he'd probably tell Benny that someone was looking for him.

If I waited long enough, he'd probably lead me straight to Golson. But first, I had to pretend I was leaving.

I walked out the door of the laundromat. I turned right, walked down the block, then crossed the street. Then I doubled back until I was right across the street from the laundromat.

I stepped inside a used-book store. There was a rack of books by the front window. I picked up a book and pretended to leaf through it. Every now and then, I looked through the window at the laundromat.

I hadn't turned more than a few pages when the boy walked out the laundromat door. He looked up and down the street, then set off to his left.

I gave him a head start, then followed. We went down two more streets and across a parking lot. I saw him go into

*I was right across the street
from the laundromat.*

an old, brown house on Lafayette Street.

It seemed to be some sort of a rooming house, just the sort of place where Golson would live. I went up the steps. The front door wasn't locked, and I pushed my way through.

Inside, the hall was dark and quiet. The kid was coming back toward the front door.

He almost walked into my arms before he looked up and saw me. He turned to run away, but I grabbed him. I picked him up, turned him around, and pinned him against the wall.

"Where's Golson?" I growled. I put my face up against his as I said it, and I shook him.

His eyes opened wide. He pointed a finger as best he could.

"One–C," he mumbled.

I dropped him and walked to the door of 1–C. I knocked.

A voice from inside said, "Yes?"

"I know you're in there, Benny," I said. "I want to talk to you."

"Certainly," the voice answered. "I'll be right there."

I waited a few seconds. The door stayed closed. Then I heard the sound of wood squeaking against wood.

I turned and raced down the hall, heading to the rear of the building. There was a back door. I threw it open and managed to run down the crooked wooden steps without breaking my leg.

Benny was climbing out of the window of his room. He was a short, round man in a red-checked suit. He fell from the window into the dirt.

Then he got up and took off across the back lot, his short legs pumping. I hit

Benny was climbing out of the window of his room.

him with a flying tackle.

"I didn't do it!" he shouted. "I want to see my lawyer! I can pay it back!"

He was kicking and trying to roll away from me. I pulled myself up so I had one knee in the small of his back. I pulled one of his arms behind him and up against his shoulder.

With my free hand, I pulled the letter from the law firm out of my pocket. I flipped it open and held it in front of Benny's face.

The kicking slowed down as he read the letter. Then, finally, it stopped.

I got up, then he got up. We dusted ourselves off. Benny had a tear in his eye.

"Dear old Uncle Milford," he said.

"You were fond of him?" I asked.

"Never met the man," Benny said. He squared his shoulders. "But I guess now it's up to me to carry on the family business."

He started back to his room, then stopped. "By the way," he said, "you wouldn't be interested in buying a ticket to the Firefighter's Ball, would you?"